DOMITILLE DE PRESSENSÉ

Emily's Letters

Letters from Emily to James

For Erwan

KINGFISHER BOOKS

Kingfisher Books, Grisewood & Dempsey Ltd,
Elsley House, 24-30 Great Titchfield Street,
London W1P 7AD

First published in this edition in the UK
in 1989 by Kingfisher Books
Originally published in France in 1982 by
Rouge et Or under the title Le Grand Livre D'Émilie

BRITISH LIBRARY CATALOGUING IN PUBLICATION DATA
De Pressensé, Domitille
  Emily's Letters
  I. Title   II. Series.   III. Le grand livre d'Émilie.
  English
  843'.914 [J]
  ISBN 0 86272 488 0

Translated by Philip Gibbs
Edited by Jackie Dobbyne
Phototypeset by Turner Typesetting
Printed in Spain

Hello!
I am Emily.

I live in a house
near a wood

with Mummy,
Daddy, Stephen
and Alice,

and my pet
hedgehog,
Arthur.

I have a bear
with one leg,

and a little
green chair.

Here are my
cousins, Simon,
Joe and Jack...

and this is my
cousin Harriet.

I have a friend
who lives far
away.

His name is
James

and I like him
very much.

He always comes
to stay with us
at Christmas,

and we play
together all the
time.

When he has to
go home, we are
both very sad.

But this year, we
had an idea: while
we wait for next

Christmas, we
shall write letters
to each other...

After winter... comes spring

January

February

March

January

Dear James

   This morning, we were all very sad because you have gone home.

   Mummy told us to go outside and build a snowman. But we didn't really want to.

   Then we had a good idea: we built a "snow James" and pretended you were still here.

   We collected twigs from

January

the fir tree for your hair and used a carrot for your nose. Mummy and Daddy said it was a very good snow James. They said it looked just like you.

We put him in the cart
and danced around him.
Daddy took our photograph.
I am sending it to you.
With love from
Emily

Dear Emily

What a good idea to build a snow James! Thank you for the photo. I have pinned it up in my bedroom next to the painting I drew today with the box of paints you gave me for Christmas.

Love from
James

Dear James

   The sun has come out
and melted the snow
James. I am sad because
we cannot play with him
any more.

   Yesterday we went for a
long walk and I drew a
picture of what we saw. I
hope you like it.

   Lots of love
   Emily

March

1

2

3

4

5

March

6

7

8

9

10

After spring... comes summer

April

May

June

Dear Emily

I am sending you this photograph of me standing in front of my house so that you will remember me even though the snow James has melted.

April

Today is a holiday and my three friends Lucy, Thomas and William came to play.

We played games in the garden and I was the winner of hide-and-seek.

After tea, we all wrote letters. I wrote mine to you. Then Mummy gave us balloons on strings and we tied the letters to them.

We let the balloons float up into the sky. My balloon is red

April

April

but I don't know if it will ever reach your house because you live such a long way away.
Love from
James

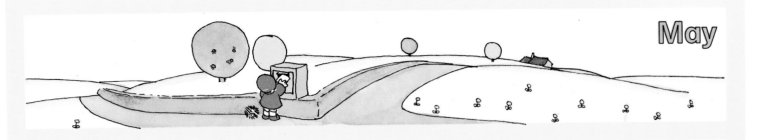

Dear James

 Your balloon hasn't arrived yet. I wonder where it is? I look out for it every day. Perhaps it has floated the wrong way!

 Last night I had a strange dream about it. I dreamed I saw your balloon floating across the garden.

May

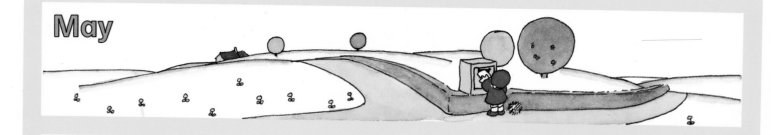

So I chased it, but I fell over with a bump! Then I woke up...
I had fallen out of bed!
Lots of love
Emily

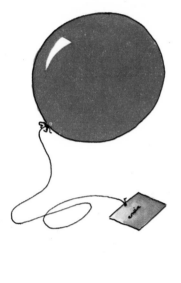

Hello, Emily!

Keep looking for the balloon. I'm sure it will arrive soon.

Today Daddy and I made a picture alphabet. I am sending it to you.

With love from
James

Aa

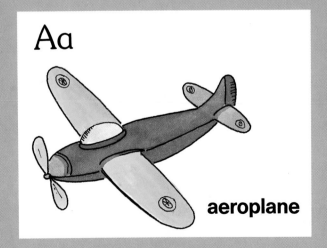

aeroplane

Bb

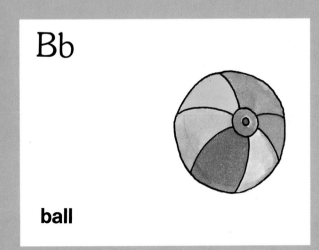

ball

June

Cc

castle

Dd

doll

Ee

elephant

Ff

flowers

Gg

gloves

Hh

hedgehog

June

Ii

island

Jj

juice

Kk

koala

Ll

lion

Mm

merry-go-round

Nn

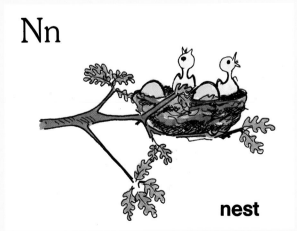

nest

June

Oo
oranges

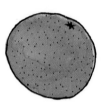

Pp
pear

Qq
queues

Rr

radishes

Ss
snake

Tt
train

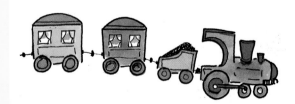

June

Uu

urn

Vv

violets

Ww

wagon

Xx

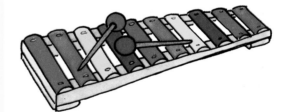

xylophone

Yy

yacht

Zz

zebra

After summer...
comes autumn

July

August

September

Dear James

I have been looking up at the sky but I still can't see your balloon. It is hard to look at the sky because the sun is so bright.

Yesterday it was really hot. Daddy filled the tub so that we could cool down in the water. We all climbed in, and the water spilled out over the sides.

July

It was very funny. We got out of the tub because there was no water left inside. We shall fill it up again tomorrow.

Love and kisses

Emily

Dear Emily

I'm sorry my balloon hasn't arrived yet. Perhaps it will come back to my house. Just in case, I stand in the garden every day and look up at the sky. Mummy says I look very funny.

I still hope my balloon will reach you soon.

Lots of love

James

Dear James

Your last letter made
Stephen laugh. He says
that, if I always have my
nose in the air looking for
the balloon, I will have
lots of accidents. He has
drawn pictures of them
for you.

Lots of love

Emily

Here is Emily,
trying to catch the balloon

September

Emily tore her dress on Monday

Slipped into the pond on Tuesday

Fell into the sea on Wednesday

Broke all her toys on Thursday

Was carried away by the wind on Friday

Was fed up with all that on Saturday

And hoped it wouldn't happen again on Sunday

September

Monday

Tuesday

Wednesday

Thursday

Friday

Saturday

Sunday

After autumn...
comes winter

October

November

December

Dear Emily

I thought the balloon might have come back to my house during the night. So I looked on top of the logs, and at the bottom of the steps, under the tree and on the pile of sand...

...and suddenly, in the grass, I saw
something red like the balloon...
but it was only a mushroom!
    With lots of love
    James

November

Dear James

Last night, I cried in bed. I thought the balloon was lost and that it would never reach my house.

Daddy gave me a big hug and said that, if I wished hard, I would soon have lots of balloons. I hope so.

Love and kisses
Emily

Dear Emily

Here is a Christmas card that I made specially for you. Mummy helped me, but only a little.

By the time you receive this card, I shall be on my way to your house. Don't worry if my balloon has not arrived as I shall bring you lots and lots of them.

Love and kisses
James

December

Merry Christmas

Emily is happy.

It is almost
Christmas.
James is coming.

The bell rings.

Emily opens
the door.

There is
no one there.

It is snowing
and it is dark.

But... there is
a balloon in the
garden,

and another,
and another, and
more over there.

James is here!

James has come back!